For my family and friends, with love

First published in the United States of America in November 2016 by Bloomsbury Children's Books
www.bloomsbury.com

Bloomsbury is a registered trademark of Bloomsbury Publishing Plc

For information about permission to reproduce selections from this book, write to Permissions, Bloomsbury Children's Books, 1385 Broadway, New York, New York 10018
Bloomsbury books may be purchased for business or promotional use. For information on bulk purchases please contact
Macmillan Corporate and Premium Sales Department at specialmarkets@macmillan.com

Library of Congress Cataloging-in-Publication Data
Names: Rankin, Laura, author, illustrator.
Title: My turn! / by Laura Rankin.
Description: New York : Bloomsbury, 2016.
Summary: Best friends Pammy and Wyatt argue because Pammy always gets her way, but after shooting baskets with her older brother, she is ready to give Wyatt a turn.
Identifiers: LCCN 2015040000 | ISBN 978-1-59990-174-9 (hardcover)
Subjects: | CYAC: Best friends—Fiction. | Friendship—Fiction. | Fairness—Fiction. | Play—Fiction. | Sheep—Fiction. | Goats—Fiction. | BISAC: JUVENILE FICTION/
Social Issues/Manners & Etiquette. | JUVENILE FICTION/Social Issues/Friendship. | JUVENILE FICTION/Imagination & Play.
Classification: LCC PZ7.R16825 My 2016 | DDC [E]—dc23 | LC record available at https://lccn.loc.gov/2015040000

Illustrations created with pen and ink, watercolor, and colored pencil on Arches 140 lb. cold press watercolor paper
Typeset in Horley Old Style and Zemke Hand • Book design by Colleen Andrews
Printed in China by Leo Paper Products, Heshan, Guangdong
1 3 5 7 9 10 8 6 4 2

All papers used by Bloomsbury Publishing, Inc., are natural, recyclable products made from wood grown in well-managed forests.
The manufacturing processes conform to the environmental regulations of the country of origin.

My Turn!

Laura Rankin

BLOOMSBURY

NEW YORK   LONDON   OXFORD   NEW DELHI   SYDNEY

Every day, my best friend, Wyatt,
and I hang out together.

Inside . . .

or outside . . .
we always have fun.

Today, we had a parade.
I got to ride in the float.

Wyatt and I love parades.
I'm always the queen.

After that, we went on the swing.

Getting dizzy helps me think up more fun stuff for us to do.

We played my favorite game.
Wyatt likes it when I'm the teacher.

But today, Wyatt didn't want to play by the rules.
Instead, he got all mad.

I don't know what happened.
I thought we were having fun.

I went to see what my brother, Eddie, was up to.

Eddie is really good at it.

The game was really boring . . .

And then I remembered . . .

Hey, Wyatt!